This book
belongs to

....

Puddle's Fan Pages

Here's what other children have to say about their favourite puppy and his friends!

"I always like it when Puddle licks people. It was funny when they turned tiny. I loved reading it, like all of the books." Lydia, age 7

"Puddle is naughty but very cute. Ruby is so kind and I really liked her idea to make a necklace for Alberto so he could be seen and make friends. This is a cool story." Ava, age 7

"I personally think the book is great!!! I like the way when they jump into the puddle they appear on a banana leaf and have been shrunken."
Florence, age 7

"I hope my visit to my Granny and Grandad's this summer is as exciting as Ruby's trip to her grandad's!" Megan, age 6

"Ruby is so adventurous . . . I wish she could be my best friend!" Ella, age 7

"I would love to have a puppy like Puddle, who could take me to different places and we could have adventures together." Kyla, age 6

Puddle
the naughtiest puppy

Rainforest
Hide and Seek

Puddle
the naughtiest puppy

Rainforest
Hide and Seek

by Hayley Daze
illustrated by James Mitchell
cover illustrated by Paul Hardman

A catalogue record for this book is available from the British Library

Published by Ladybird Books Ltd MMX
A Penguin Company
Penguin Books Ltd., 80 Strand, London WC2R oRL, UK
Penguin Books Australia Ltd., Camberwell, Victoria, Australia
Penguin Group (NZ) 67 Apollo Drive, Rosedale,
North Shore 0632, New Zealand

2

Series created by Working Partners Limited, London WC1X 9HH
Text © Working Partners Ltd MMX

Special thanks to Jane Clarke

ISBN: 978-1-40930-330-5
Printed in England

Mixed Sources
Product group from well-managed
forests and other controlled sources
www.fsc.org   Cert no. SA-COC-001592
© 1996 Forest Stewardship Council

FSC

To Amy, Aaliyah and Chloe

When clouds fill the sky and rain starts to fall,
Ruby and Harry are not sad at all.
They know that when puddles appear on the ground,
A magical puppy will soon be around!

Puddle's his name, and he's the one
Who can lead you to worlds of adventure and fun!
He may be quite naughty, but he's clever too,
So come follow Puddle – he's waiting for you!

A present from Puddle:

Look out for the special code at the back of the book to
get extra-special games and loads of free stuff at Puddle's
website! Come and play at www.puddlethepuppy.com

Contents

Chapter One
Making a Splash

"I'm a water fairy!" Ruby cried,
wrapping a damp strand of feathery
pondweed around her head and
sticking a pink water lily behind
one ear. "And I can make
myself invisible."

Her plaits bounced
as she waved her
fishing net like a

magic wand. Ruby's cousin Harry stared at her.

"I can still see you," he said, pushing his glasses up his nose. He lifted his fishing net out of Grandad's pond and peered into it. "I've caught something!" he exclaimed.

"Let me look." Ruby raced over to Harry and peered inside the bulging, dripping net. "It's just lots of pondweed and tiny bits of sticks and stone," she said.

But then the pondweed moved. A little green frog sitting among the leaves began to ribbet.

"Wow!" Ruby said. "He's the exact same colour as the pondweed."

"It's called camouflage," Harry said. He flicked through his favourite wildlife book, which was lying open at the pond-life page. "Lots of creatures use it to blend in with their surroundings, so no one can see them."

"Like they're invisible," Ruby said, smiling.

Ruby and Harry carefully tipped the frog on to a lily pad. Ruby's

pondweed crown fell off as she lay on her tummy at the edge of the pond and watched the frog hop from leaf to leaf. Two electric-blue dragonflies whizzed and hovered overhead. Then a series of ripples spread out across the water.

Plop, plop ... plop, plop ... plop.

Ruby's heart leapt with joy. Huge raindrops were plopping into the pond, bouncing off the lily pads. Water dripped from her plaits as she sat up. "Where's Puddle?" she asked.

Whenever it rained, their naughty puppy friend arrived, and they went on magical adventures.

On the far side of the pond, a clump

of rushes rustled.

"Woof! Woof!" Puddle bounded
out of the rushes towards Ruby and
Harry, wagging his tail. Ruby and
Harry's wellies were in his mouth.

"Hello, boy," Ruby said, patting
Puddle all over. "Where are you
taking us today?"

The little puppy trotted up the garden path, where the rain had already made large puddles. Ruby held her breath. When Puddle was around, a rainy puddle could become the gateway to a new and exciting adventure. Puddle stopped at the largest pool of water, ran round it, jumped in – and disappeared.

Ruby turned to Harry and shouted, "One, two, three, JUMP!"

And into the puddle they went.

Chapter Two
Rainforest Magic

When Ruby opened her eyes, she was floating down a muddy river. The warm air echoed with strange squawking, hooting and ribbeting noises. Above her, she could make out the shape of enormous individual trees, hung with thick leafy vines. Some of them trailed in the water.

"Where are we?" she asked.

Harry scratched his head. "Let me see. The climate's warm and wet, and lots of plants and animals live here . . . I know – we're in a rainforest!" he said, a wide smile on his face. "I've always wanted to visit one."

"Me too." Ruby tingled all over with excitement. She took hold of Puddle's front paws and bounced him up and down. The river lapped around them. "Are we on some kind

of a boat?" she asked Harry.

He knelt down to inspect it, then his eyes widened with surprise. He pointed to the cluster of huge, curved, yellow objects floating behind them. "We're on an enormous banana leaf." He shook his head. "It can't be possible."

"But those bananas are big enough for giants to eat," Ruby said. "Are we in a giant's rainforest?"

Squawk! said something above them. An enormous parrot with a blue-and-yellow body and scarlet wing feathers flew over their heads.

Ruby gasped. "The parrot's as big as a pony!" she said.

"We're not in a giant's rainforest," said Harry slowly. "We've shrunk!"

Ruby gave a shout of delight and hugged Puddle to her as she skipped up and down the banana leaf. "Small enough to dance with a monkey, or teeny-tiny enough to ride on the back of a hummingbird?" she asked excitedly.

Harry counted on his fingers as he did some calculations. "Well, the parrot was pony-size, and the bananas are giant-size, so I think we must be frog-size."

"Frog-size is a lovely size to be," Ruby said. She ruffled Puddle's ears. "That makes Puddle tadpole-size."

As they floated downriver on the banana leaf, Ruby thought how

wonderful it was to be so tiny. The
rainforest animals weren't bothered
by them at all. An enormous green
lizard with a frilled neck, which
was sunning itself on the riverbank,
stared curiously as the banana leaf
floated past.

"Look, Harry!" cried Ruby, as
a group of chattering monkeys
skipped through the lush trees that
grew on the banks. She saw a flash of
movement in the water, close to their

banana leaf. "Those fish have got horrible teeth," she said.

"Wow," Harry said. "They're piranhas. I read all about rainforest creatures in my wildlife book. They can gobble up anything that falls into the river in seconds."

Zzzzzzzzzz! A neon-blue bug the size of Puddle landed on the bunch of bananas at the end of their leaf. The little puppy sprinted up the leaf towards it. The bug took off and zipped all around them, Puddle jumping after it.

"Puddle's going to fall in the river," Harry shouted.

"Where the piranhas are," Ruby added. "Stop, Puddle!"

But the puppy carried on running. Ruby and Harry chased Puddle, and Puddle chased the giant bug. One of Puddle's paws slipped from the banana leaf into the water. He wobbled on the edge, and Ruby flung herself at him, just catching him before he fell into the river. Harry

landed in a heap on top of them.
Puddle squirmed in Ruby's arms,
yapping at the giant blue bug as it
zoomed off.

"Naughty Puddle," Ruby said.
Then she saw that Harry's face was
pale.

The commotion had disturbed the
water around the banana leaf – and
the piranhas were staring straight at
them, their sharp teeth glinting.

Chapter Three
River Ride

"We need to get away from them,"
Harry cried, as the piranhas snapped
their teeth. His eyes were wide with
fear behind his glasses.

"But how?" asked Ruby, clutching
Puddle to her. "If only we could make
the banana leaf go faster."

Puddle whined miserably.

"The bananas!" Harry shouted.

He ran across the leaf to where the massive yellow fruit bobbed along behind them, attached to the leaf by a brown stalk. "It's all a matter of physics. If we can pull the leaf away from the bananas, it won't weigh so much. Then we'll go faster."

"You're a genius!" Ruby said. She tugged on her plaits for luck, and

she and Harry pulled at the stalk
between the leaf and the bananas.
Even Puddle nibbled it with his teeth.
The leaf broke free, and with a *whoosh*
it raced down the river, away from the
piranhas.

"We did it!" said Ruby, hugging
Puddle. She smiled as her plaits
streamed out behind her. "I like
going fast!" Then her face fell. She
pointed a shaking finger at two fins
sticking out of the water. "Sharks!"

35

"No – river dolphins," Harry said. "They're friendly. See?"

The river dolphins leapt playfully and rolled about in the water. Then they stopped frolicking, nudged the banana leaf gently with their beaky noses, turned and swam upstream.

"Don't go!" Ruby called.

The water was picking up speed, swirling and rushing around the banana leaf, which went even faster.

"The river is too fast for the river dolphins now," Harry said, clutching the side of the leaf.

"It's too fast for me, too!" Ruby cried. Puddle jumped from Ruby's lap and raced from side to side, yipping at the bubbling water.

"Oh, Puddle, no!" Harry shouted over the roar of the river. Their banana-leaf boat rocked as the little puppy scampered across the leaf and skidded to a stop near the leaf's edge. The banana leaf bounced off a rock and spun round wildly, rolling back and forth in the foaming white water.

Ruby scooped Puddle into her arms. "You've turned our river ride into a rollercoaster," Ruby whispered to Puddle, cuddling him close.

"There are rapids ahead!" Harry's knuckles went pale as he clutched the edge of the leaf. "Hold tight!" he yelled.

Ruby's ears were filled with a

roaring, rushing, crashing noise.
Puddle began to howl.

"It's a waterfall!" Ruby gasped.
"We're going to be swept over it!"

Chapter Four
Rainforest Rescue

"This way! This way!" something squawked over the noise of the rushing water.

A toucan with gorgeous glossy dark feathers and a huge orangey-yellow beak was flying above their banana-leaf boat. It swooped down the

right-hand fork of the river and flew
off into the rainforest.

"All lean to the right!" Ruby yelled.

They rushed to the right of the
banana leaf, steering it so that it
swung towards the right fork. They
clung on desperately as the leaf
whizzed down a flume of water, and
landed with a tremendous splash in a
crystal-clear pool.

Ruby shook the water from her plaits and looked back. Her mouth fell open. The other fork of the river would have taken them crashing straight over a cascading waterfall.

They floated gently downstream until, ahead of them, the pool widened into a shallow lake carpeted with gigantic emerald-green lily pads.

"Look at the frogs," Ruby said. The banana leaf rocked as she jumped up and down, pointing ahead to a group of glistening frogs sitting on the lily pads. The frogs were all different colours – shiny red, yellow, blue, purple, orange and green – and they were ribbeting to each other as the banana leaf floated closer. "You were

right, Harry," she said. "We are frog-size – those frogs are as big as we are!"

"I hope they're friendly," Harry said nervously.

The banana leaf bumped gently into the closest lily pad, where a sunshine-yellow frog was sitting. It blinked at them.

"Woof!" Puddle bounded on to the other lily pad and into the frog, knocking it over. He gave it a big, sloppy lick.

"Puddle!" Ruby called. "We're sorry," she said to the frog. "Puddle's naughty sometimes, but he's just trying to be friendly."

The frog made a giggling, ribbety sound. "I'm Frida," she croaked, "and these are my friends, the Rainforest Ribbeters."

"Hello, Frida," Ruby said. "I'm Ruby, this is my cousin Harry – and you've already met Puddle."

Puddle looked up at the shiny frog and wagged his tail.

"What are the Rainforest Ribbeters?" Harry asked.

"The Rainforest Ribbeters are a team," Frida said. Her shiny yellow face was hopeful. "Have you seen our ball?" she asked. "It's a special bouncy ball made from sticky rubber-tree sap."

Harry shook his head.

Frida's froggy shoulders sagged. "It took us ages to make," she croaked. "And it was perfect for Lily Pad Ping-pong."

"We'll help you find it," Ruby told Frida. "We're really good at spotting things."

"This rainforest is an awful lot

bigger than Grandad's pond," Harry reminded her. "And we're very, very small."

Puddle wagged his tail.

"Puddle will help sniff it out," Ruby said confidently. "We'll find the Rainforest Ribbeters' ball in no time!"

Chapter Five
The Search Party

"Now, where did you last see your ball?" Ruby asked, rolling up her sleeves.

"On the riverbank – come with me." Frida hopped off across the lily pads, followed by the other members of the Rainforest Ribbeters.

Ruby, Harry and Puddle ran after her, making the bouncy lily pads wibble and wobble beneath their feet. Ruby and Harry kept falling over, but ahead of them, Puddle was bouncing along on his back legs.

"Puddle's got the right idea," Ruby said, puffing and using a plait to wipe her face. "He's hopping like the frogs. Let's copy Puddle!" She held both hands out in front of her and began to bounce up and down. "Wheeeeee!

This is fun!" she squealed, launching herself into the air.

Boing ... boing ... boing ...

Ruby, Harry and Puddle bounced from pad to pad and soon caught up with the frogs. They landed with a squelch in the mud on the riverbank.

A garden of beautiful pink orchids was growing between the roots of tall vine-covered rainforest trees. A bird with an enormous orangey-yellow beak was rummaging between the orchids' waxy petals.

"I think that's the toucan who saved us from the waterfall," Ruby told Harry.

"Hey, Nico," Frida called to the

toucan. "Have you seen our ball?"

"No," Nico told Frida, in a squawk that was muffled by orchid petals. "I'm looking for my favourite shell."

"Which one's that?" asked Frida.

"The one with the shiny inside,

where you can see a reflection of
yourself pulling funny faces," Nico
said. "It's disappeared." He lifted his
beak out of the flowers.

"Hello!" he squawked at Ruby,
Harry and Puddle. "Where have I
seen you before?"

Before Ruby or Harry could
answer, Puddle yipped and
scampered up to Nico, licking
his beak.

Ruby ran forward and scooped Puddle into her arms before he could knock Nico over. "We're Ruby and Harry, and this is Puddle, a very naughty puppy."

"You saved us, Nico," Harry said to the toucan. "We're the people who were floating down the river."

"You're very small for people," Nico squawked, tilting his head to one side.

"We may be small, but we can help you find your shell," Ruby told him. "We're already helping the frogs look for their ball."

Harry scratched his head. "It's strange that the ball and the shell have gone missing," he said. "Maybe someone's taken them."

"Woof! Woof!" Puddle jumped from Ruby's arms and began to snuffle around, busily wagging his tail. A loop of vine leaves and orchid petals got caught around him as he rummaged through the undergrowth.

"That's a pretty necklace, Puddle," Ruby said, chuckling. "You blend in so well with the rainforest, I can hardly see you."

"Let's camouflage ourselves,
too," Harry said. "Then we can spot
whoever's got the ball and the shell
without being seen." He pulled down
a creeper and draped it loosely round
his shoulders.

"My legs need camouflage," Ruby
said, stuffing rubbery leaves into
the tops of her wellies to hide her
leggings. "Now, let's find whoever's

taken the missing things. Maybe they're inside one of the flowers." She peered into a huge pink orchid filled with sweet-smelling nectar. The ends of her plaits came out very sticky.

Ruby, Harry and Puddle clambered over the enormous gnarly tree roots, pushing aside the cool, glossy green leaves of the vines that hung down from the trees, and sticking their noses into every flower they found.

"What are you sss . . . searching for?" hissed a voice above them. Ruby looked up in surprise. The voice was coming from a red snake coiled round a tree branch. Puddle's tail stopped wagging and he began to whimper.

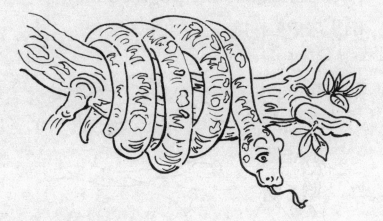

"There's one rainforest creature Puddle doesn't want to lick," Harry whispered, as the puppy hid behind his legs.

"That's our friend Rosa. She won't hurt you," Frida told them.

"Hello, Rosa!" Ruby called nervously. She'd never spoken to a snake before. "We're looking for Nico's shell and the frogs' bouncy ball."

"Gone mi ... sss ... sing, have they?" Rosa uncoiled, keeping the end of her tail wrapped around the branch, and swung down so that her head was level with Ruby's. "Lotsss of thingsss are going miss…sss…sing around here. I hope I don't lose my sss…sparkly sss…stone."

Rosa glanced back up to her branch. Next to her tail, an egg-shaped gemstone twinkled in the sunshine.

"It's a diamond," Harry gasped. "I read that you can find diamonds in the rainforest."

"You should take good care of that, Rosa," Ruby said. But as she spoke, there was a blur of movement on Rosa's branch. Something long, thin and pink whipped out of the leaves and stuck to Rosa's sparkly stone.

In a flash, the diamond and the long pink thing disappeared into the rainforest!

Chapter Six
Rainforest Detectives

"My sss . . . stone!" Rosa hissed in dismay. "I've got to get it back! When the sss . . . sun shines through it, it makes rainbowsss. I let everyone use it for their partiesss."

"What happened to it?" Harry asked, pushing his glasses up his nose and looking around wildly.

"It looked like a long sssticky –

I mean sticky – tongue," Ruby said slowly, gazing through the vine leaves, up into the tree. "But there's no sign of the body it belongs to."

Suddenly, Puddle froze. He was staring at a hole in the tree trunk, a little way above one of the great roots that supported the tree. His ears pricked up.

He yapped.

Ruby followed the little puppy's gaze. The bark on the tree trunk was moving. It went still for a moment, then a long pink tongue darted into a clump of white orchids growing next to the entrance to the hole.

"Something's lapping up the

nectar," Ruby whispered to Harry. "What is it? Its body is invisible."

"There's only one way to find out," Harry said. "It must live in that hole. We're small and we're wearing camouflage. It won't see us coming."

Frida whispered, "It would see the Rainforest Ribbeters. And Nico and Rosa. We'd better stay here."

"Good idea," Ruby told her. "It's hard to hide when you're so brightly coloured."

Puddle hunched down and crawled towards the tree under the cover of the vine leaves.

"Puddle's got the right idea," Harry whispered to Ruby. They followed

Puddle's lead, dropping to all fours and creeping up the tree root towards the mysterious creature's home. As quietly as they could, they hauled themselves up on the tree bark and peered inside the hole.

There, right in front of their eyes, was Rosa's huge sparkly diamond.

Ruby stuck her head in further. Her reflection stared back at her, but with a wobbly smile and wonky plaits. It looked so funny that Ruby couldn't help laughing. She realized she was looking at herself reflected in Nico's shiny shell.

Something rustled at the back of the hole.

Ruby's heart thumped as she stared into the darkness. She could make out a ball that looked as if it was made of sticky rubber bands. And, right at the back of the hole, there was a bright green scaly creature with bulgy eyes like marbles. It was licking its lips with its long pink tongue. Ruby's eyes opened wide and a shiver ran down her spine.

"It's a dragon!" she squealed. "A dragon thief!"

The dragon-like creature's bulgy eyes swivelled towards Ruby, Harry and Puddle. Then, in an instant, the creature was gone. Puddle barked in amazement.

"It disappeared!" Ruby gasped. "Right before our eyes."

Chapter Seven
The Trouble
with Camouflage

"It's still there," Harry said slowly.
"Look again."

Ruby peered into the hole until her
eyes got used to the dark. Harry was
right. The creature was there, only his
scales had turned as dark as the hole.

"It is a dragon," she whispered.
"And it's bigger than we are. What if
it tries to eat us?"

"It's only a chameleon," Harry said, grinning. "Chameleons are a kind of lizard that can change colour to hide themselves. They're experts at camouflage."

Ruby stared at the chameleon. The chameleon's eyes opened wide and it shivered with fear. Ruby knew just how it felt.

"H . . . hello, Chameleon," she said in her gentlest voice. "It's okay. We're not going to hurt you. What's your name?"

"Al ... Alberto." The chameleon's scales flushed pink as he answered Ruby.

"We just want to know why you took these things, Alberto," Ruby told him. "They don't belong to you, do they?"

"N ... n ... no." Alberto's scales turned pale green and his googly eyes swivelled downwards with shame.

"I just wanted to play with them for a while. No one ever plays with me," he sighed.

Puddle seemed to realize that Alberto was unhappy. He wriggled into the hole, but instead of licking the chameleon or sending him flying, he curled up quietly next to him.

"Poor Alberto!" Ruby said. "It must be horrible to be so lonely."

"It is," the chameleon sniffed. His scales changed to the colour of Puddle's fur, so he looked like a furry lizard. "No one in the rainforest ever seems to notice me."

"We can see what the problem is," Harry said, looking over the top of his glasses at Ruby. She nodded. Puddle barked.

"We'll help you," Ruby told Alberto. "But it wasn't nice to take those things. The creatures who own them are very upset."

"I'm sorry," Alberto said, turning pink so that they could see the tears

glistening in his bulgy eyes. "I was
going to give them back."

"That's okay, Alberto," said Ruby.
"We can do it right now."

Ruby, Harry and Puddle scrambled
down the tree root.

"Look what we've found!" Ruby
yelled to the waiting rainforest
creatures. Frida and the frogs
hopped, Nico fluttered and Rosa
slithered over to the base of the tree.

Alberto poked his head out of his hole and his scales instantly went the colour of the bark.

"Brilliant camouflage," Harry murmured admiringly.

"I know where Alberto is, and I can hardly see him," Ruby said in amazement as the chameleon took the treasures out of his hole.

Ruby, Harry and Puddle watched the rainforest creatures' eyes widen with astonishment as a shiny shell, a bouncy ball and a sparkly stone fell from the tree. Puddle caught each in his mouth and returned it to its owner.

"Yippee!" Rosa, Nico, Frida and the Rainforest Ribbeters yelled as they held their treasures.

"They haven't spotted Alberto yet," Harry whispered to Ruby as the cheering died away and Alberto scrambled down the tree root. "He's still invisible to them."

They watched as Alberto took a deep breath. "I'm so sorry I took your things," he announced in a slow, soft voice.

The rainforest creatures looked around in surprise.

"I didn't know trees could talk," Frida gasped.

"It's not a talking tree – it's Alberto. He's a chameleon," Harry explained. "No one ever sees him because his camouflage is so good."

"Alberto didn't mean any harm," Ruby added quickly. "He just wants to be friends. He's lonely because he hasn't got anyone to play with."

"We didn't mean to leave you out, Alberto," Frida croaked. "It's just hard to ask someone to play when you don't know where they are."

"Being invisible all the time isn't much fun," Alberto sighed.

Ruby turned to Harry and Puddle.

They were still wearing creepers and flowers around their shoulders.

"It sounds like Alberto needs the opposite of camouflage," she said, looking round at the rainforest. "Now, what can a chameleon wear when he wants to be seen?"

Chapter Eight
Hide and Seek

"Woof! Woof! Woof!" Puddle raced about, pulling mouthfuls of vines from the surrounding trees.

"Cut that out, Puddle," Harry scolded. Puddle jumped up at Ruby, snagging her leggings.

Ruby shook her head at what the naughty puppy had done. The vines clenched in Puddle's jaws tickled Ruby's legs.

Ruby rubbed the puppy's head. "Oh, I understand, Puddle. He's trying to help," she told the others. "Sorry, Puddle, but I think putting these vines on Alberto will make him more camouflaged than ever."

"Alberto needs something that stands out," said Harry. "Something shiny and colourful."

"Woof!" Puddle dropped the pile of vines at Ruby's feet. He shook his body as if he'd just been given a bath. A bright pink orchid petal flew off his back.

Ruby gazed at it thoughtfully. "That's it, Puddle!" Ruby exclaimed. "You're a genius." Ruby grabbed a vine and started to strip off the leaves. "We can use some vine stems to make a necklace for Alberto. Hold the ends, Puddle, while I plait them."

The frogs, Nico, Rosa and Alberto looked puzzled as Puddle held the vines firmly in his mouth. Ruby plaited them into a circle and made sure it fitted over Alberto's head. "Now we have to cover it with bright colourful things," she told the others.

"I'll pick some flowers," Harry said.

"I'll find some shiny shells," Nico

squawked, flapping off.

"And I've got lotsss of sss ... small sss ... sparkly sss ... stones," Rosa hissed. "I'll go and fetch them."

"What can we do?" Frida croaked.

Ruby pointed to the Rainforest Ribbeters' sticky bouncy ball. "We need a little bit of something sticky to glue it all together," she said.

Soon Alberto's necklace was complete.

Ruby stood with her hands on her hips and admired their handiwork. The sap from the frogs' ball had stuck everything on beautifully. The plaited circle of vines was covered in brightly coloured orchids, glittering shells and tiny stones that sparkled in the sunlight. It was so beautiful that Ruby wished she had a rainforest necklace too.

"This is from all of your new friends," Ruby said, fitting the necklace over Alberto's neck. The chameleon turned red with pleasure.

"Thank you," he said to everyone. "It's perfect!"

"What are you going to play, now you can all play together?" Harry asked.

"How about a game of hide and seek?" Ruby suggested.

"I won't take off my necklace," Alberto promised with a grin.

Frida, Nico and Rosa laughed. "That's good," they said.

"Yip, yip, yip!" Puddle wagged his tail and ran in a circle round Ruby and Harry.

"It's time for us to go home now,"
Ruby told their rainforest friends.
"Have fun!"

"We will!" Frida croaked. She
closed her eyes and began to count.

"One ... two ... three ..."

Alberto and all the other rainforest
creatures scampered off to hide.

"four ... five ... six ..."

"Frida will soon spot Alberto,"
Ruby said, laughing. "I can see his
necklace!"

"seven... eight... nine..."
Puddle ran faster and faster.

"... ten!"
The rainforest became a blur of
green, and disappeared.

***

"We're still frog-size!" Ruby said in horror, staring up at the tree that towered over them. "What are we going to do?"

"It's okay," said Harry, pointing at the grass. "Those dandelions are normal size. We're under Grandad's big oak tree, so it seems like we're tiny."

"Phew," said Ruby. "Grandad would have had a big surprise – or, rather, a small one."

The sun was coming out, and the dragonflies were hovering over the water as the frogs hopped from lily pad to lily pad. Puddle raced around the pond, wagging his tail as he dashed behind the clump of rushes.

Ruby and Harry ran after him. But when they reached the rushes, Puddle had gone.

"Look," said Ruby. On the grass next to the pond was a loop of vine leaves and orchids – Puddle's rainforest necklace. Ruby put it round her shoulders.

"Do you think we've got time to play before tea?" she asked Harry.

Her cousin nodded. "Hide and seek?" he suggested with a smile.

"No peeking!" Ruby said, as she ran off to hide. To herself, she said, "Time to find some amazing camouflage!"

Can't wait to find out
what Puddle will do next?
Then read on! Here is the first
chapter from Puddle's fifth
adventure, Dragon Dance . . .

Dragon Dance

"Ready for blast-off," Ruby shouted. She held a string that stretched all the way across Grandad's garden. "In five, four, three, two..."

"Wait!" Her cousin Harry interrupted the countdown. He was holding a diamond-shaped kite that was attached to Ruby's long string. "There's just one more thing that I want to fix."

Grandad had showed them how he had made kites when he was a child. The cousins had spent all morning making a kite of their own. Ruby and Harry had used some Christmas wrapping, some tissue paper that Ruby thought matched her leggings, some comic book pages, knitting yarn, and lots of 'Well Done' stickers that Harry had saved from school.

"I want to adjust the tail so it gives us more drag," Harry called, as he pushed his glasses back into place.

"I don't want the tail to drag," Ruby said. "That'll ruin all the bows I've tied to it."

"I don't mean drag on the ground –
I mean drag as in thrust, lift and drag.
They are the forces that make the kite
fly," Harry explained.

"Come on, Harry. It's not rocket
science," Ruby teased.

"But it is rocket science ... Oh,
never mind," Harry said as he worked
on the tail. "Hey, did you know that
kites were first made in China over
two thousand years ago? They made
flying dragons and giant birds –"

"I wish I could fly like a kite," Ruby
squealed as she spread her cardigan
out like a cape and pretended to soar
around the garden.

"I don't think you'll fly," Harry

said, putting the final touches to the kite's tail, "but this will."

"Hooray," Ruby shouted. Harry held the kite up above his head as Ruby tugged on her plaits for luck.

"Blast off!" she yelled and started to run, holding on tight to the kite string. Harry let go and the kite bobbed along behind Ruby.

Then a gust of wind caught it. The kite sailed up, up and away. It dipped and swirled, doing gymnastics in the air. Ruby held on tightly as the wind tugged it higher and higher.

"It's getting away!" Ruby shouted as the string slipped through her fingers.

"Hang on!" Harry called and raced after the kite. The wind blew the kite in wild circles while the cousins chased after it.

"It's heading right for Grandad's pear tree," Harry said. "It's going to . . ." Ruby and Harry both covered their eyes ". . . crash!" Harry finished, as their kite collided with the tree.

"Oh, no!" Ruby sighed. She scrambled up the pear tree as quickly as she could.

"The kite's ripped pretty badly," she said, poking her finger though a tear in the paper at the top. She jumped down and handed Harry the kite.

"I'm sure we can fix it," Harry said,

sitting down on the grass. He tore a page out of his puzzle book, glued it over the tear and then held up the kite to examine his work.

"Let's fly it again," Ruby said, just as she felt a drop of rain on her nose. For a split second she was disappointed. They couldn't fly their kite in the rain. But then she remembered that rain always brought a magical puppy who took them on magical adventures.

"Woof! Woof!"

"Puddle!" Ruby and Harry shouted as the puppy bounded across the damp grass towards them.

Puddle barked again as he slipped

on the grass and started sliding right
in the direction of Harry and the kite!

***

To find out what happens next, get
your copy of DRAGON DANCE!
Coming soon...

Magic Carpet Ride

Join Puddle, Ruby and Harry
on their first amazing adventure!

Aziz wants to win
the magic carpet
race so he can be
granted a wish
by the beautiful
princess! Can,
Ruby, Harry and
Puddle help Aziz
to win?

Find out in MAGIC CARPET RIDE...

Toyshop Trouble

Join Puddle, Ruby and Harry
on their next exciting adventure!

This time Puddle's
magic takes them
to an amazing
toyshop. Professor
Toyjoy needs help
to win the big toy
competition!
Will Puddle be
able to save the day?

Find out in TOYSHOP TROUBLE…

Puddle
the naughtiest puppy

Ballet Show Mischief

Go on a beautiful ballet adventure
with Puddle, Ruby and Harry.

The children are
whisked away to a
wonderful ballet
show, but the shy
ballerina has stage
fright. The show
must go on! Will
Puddle be able to
find a solution?

Find out in BALLET SHOW MISCHIEF…

Dragon Dance

Join Puddle, Ruby and Harry on
their new adventure in Chinatown!

Li wants to make
his Grandad proud
by appearing in the
Chinese festival.
Can Puddle and the
children help him
to get Lucky the
dragon to dance?

Find out in DRAGON DANCE...

Puddle
the naughtiest puppy

Magic Mayhem

Ruby and Harry are amazed to find
themselves in a medieval castle...

...when Puddle
takes them on
their latest
adventure! They
meet a magician's
apprentice who is in
deep trouble. He's
lost his spell book.
Can Puddle save
the day?

Find out in MAGIC MAYHEM...

A Dog's Needs

Hi, it's Ruby and Harry again with Puddle the puppy! What a fantastic adventure we've just had. Now we are all ready to learn more about real dogs and what they need to be healthy and happy. How about you?

So today our friends from **Dogs Trust** will help us discover exactly that. After all, they look after lots and lots of real dogs and puppies each year, so they know what they are talking about.

Dogs Trust is the UK's largest dog charity and works hard to help all dogs to enjoy a happy life in a loving home.

Always remember, Puddle is a magical dog, while real dogs and puppies are living animals who need a lot of care, love and attention.

A dog needs to:

- **Eat.** Make sure that your dog has plenty of food and sometimes a treat! But never give a dog your chocolate — as it can make them very sick.
- **Drink.** Always have a fresh bowl of water on the floor.
- **Wear a collar and tag.** That way, if your dog gets lost he can be returned to you.
- **Have lots of cuddles and love.** Remember, these don't cost anything.
- **Have lots of toys to play with!**
- **Have a nice warm and comfortable bed to sleep in.** This should be just for him!
- **Have his very own lead.** That way, your dog can go on lots of safe walks with you.

Congratulations – you have started to learn about what a dog needs.

See you next time, when we will be learning about training a dog. We can't wait!

Odd Puddle Out!

Study the pictures of Puddle below and on the page opposite. One of them does not match the others! Can you spot the odd one out?

A

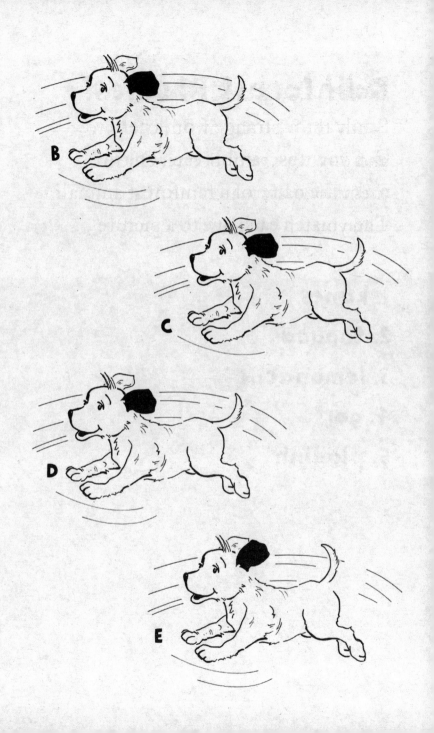

Rainforest Riddles!

Look at the strange words below.
Can you unscramble each one to
make the name of a rainforest animal?
Then match each one to a picture.

1. kanes
2. tonuca
3. lemonache
4. gorf
5. plodinh

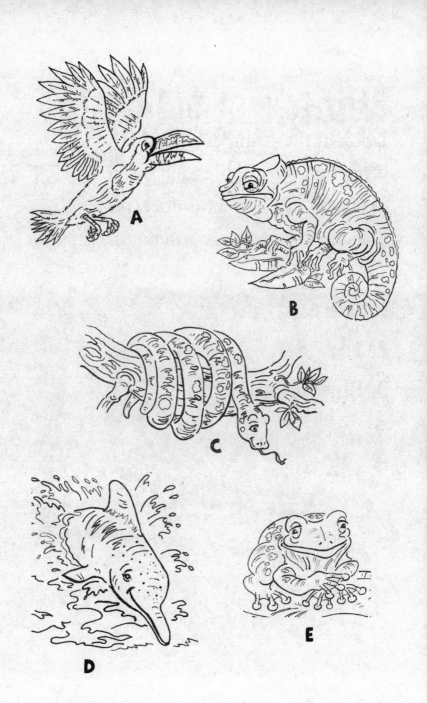

Answers to puzzles:
Odd Puddle Out! E
Rainforest Riddles! 1. snake – C, 2. toucan –A,
3. chameleon – B, 4. frog – E, 5. dolphin – D

For more magical adventures, come and play with Puddle at

www.puddlethepuppy.com

Use this special code to get extra-special games and free stuff at puddlethepuppy.com

NECKLACE